Illustrated by Jerrod Maruyama
© 2021 Disney Enterprises, Inc. All rights reserved.

Customer Service: 1-877-277-9441 or customerservice@pikidsmedia.com

Published by PI Kids, an imprint of Phoenix International Publications, Inc.

8501 West Higgins Road	59 Gloucester Place	Heimhuder Straße 81
Chicago, Illinois 60631	London W1U 8JJ	20148 Hamburg

PI Kids is a trademark of Phoenix International Publications, Inc., and is registered in the United States.

www.pikidsmedia.com

ISBN: 978-1-5037-5929-9

Huey Helps Out

A STORY ABOUT KINDNESS

pi kids ®

An imprint of Phoenix International Publications, Inc.

Chicago • London • New York • Hamburg • Mexico City • Sydney

Huey, Dewey, and Louie are playing outside when Huey gets an idea. "Look at all those boxes in the garage," he says. "What if we had a **GARAGE SALE**? We could give the money to a local charity and clean out our stuff at the same time. It's a **WIN-WIN**!"

Huey's brothers want to help the community, too. But they don't want to have a garage sale.

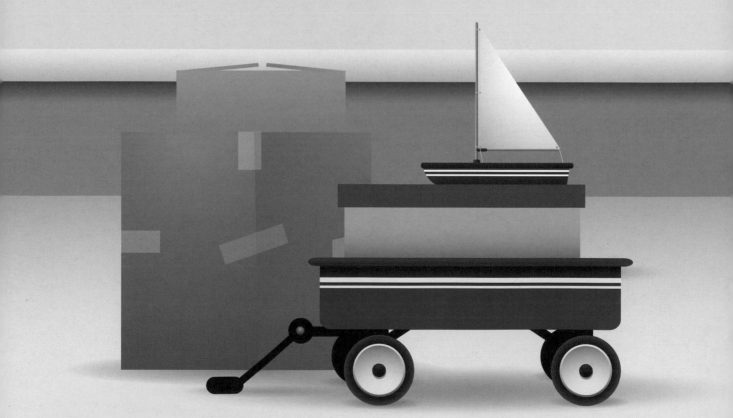

"Let's ask our friends what they think," Donald says to Huey. "I'm sure they'll want to pitch in and help when they hear your idea."

But Huey's friends all have **DIFFERENT** ideas about how to help.

"I think we should make **HERO SANDWICHES** for our **FIREFIGHTERS**," says Louie. "We can use Goofy's special recipe!"

"**HEROES** for the **HEROES!**" Goofy agrees.

Millie and Melody want to have a **BAKE SALE**.

"We'll give the money we make to the soup kitchen," says Melody. "They'll use it to feed families in need!"

"I can help!" says Mickey. "Everyone **LOVES** my chocolate chip cookies!"

But Huey would rather eat cookies than bake them.

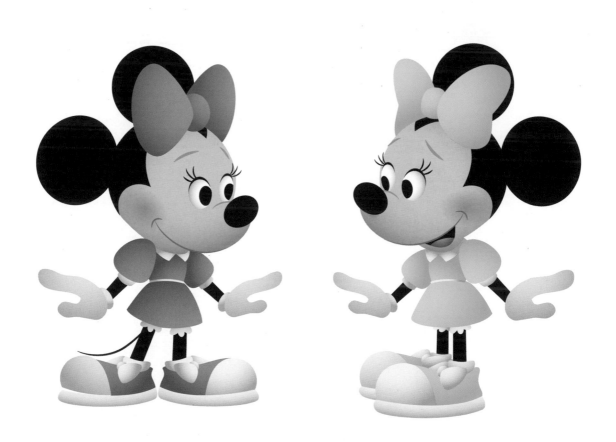

"We can sell Mickey's cookies at a **LEMONADE STAND**," says Dewey.

"That sounds like fun!" adds Louie.

"Not as much fun as a garage sale," **GRUMBLES** Huey.

HMPH!

Gilbert has *another* idea. "We could ask stores to **DONATE TOYS** and then bring them to the children's hospital," he says.

"I know all the best toy stores in town," Goofy says with a laugh.

"Wait, I have an even better idea!" says Louie. "Why don't we have a **BASKETBALL SHOOTING CONTEST**? I bet lots of kids would enter. We can ask people to donate money for every basket we make. And we can use the money to buy equipment for the after-school sports program."

"That *could* be fun," Huey admits. **"But my idea is still the best!"**

Huey and his brothers argue—until Donald blows his whistle.

"Hold on, boys," Donald says. "We've heard lots of good ideas. Let's ask everyone to **VOTE** on their favorite."

TWEET!

Huey's garage sale idea **gets ONE vote**, but the bake sale **WINS**.

Huey STOMPS his foot. "Go ahead and bake your cookies, but count me out," he says.

"I'M NOT HELPING."

"I guess we'll get started **without Huey**," Donald says. "Come on, everybody. We've got a lot of cookie baking to do!"

"And how about some pies, and tarts, and cinnamon rolls, too?" adds Goofy.

"I really LOVE cinnamon rolls," says Donald.

Donald gets to work on the dough. *Extra yeast should make it rise extra fast,* he thinks.

The dough rises quickly...**AND IT DOESN'T STOP!**

Huey runs in with a shovel and says, **"I've got this!"**

When the dough is scooped up, the friends start
on the dishes. Working together, they get the kitchen

SPARKLING CLEAN.

"Can I still work the bake sale?" asks Huey. "I like helping. It makes me feel **happy**."

"You bet," says Donald. "I'm proud of you for pitching in."

CLAP!

Then, Millie runs in with *another* idea. "What if we do **everyone's idea**?" she asks.

Melody adds, "Huey can run the GARAGE SALE.

Goofy can make HERO SANDWICHES.

Gilly can hold a TOY DRIVE.

Dewey can set up a
LEMONADE STAND.

Louie can have a
BASKETBALL SHOOTING CONTEST.

And we can have
our **BAKE SALE**.
Think of all the people
we could help!"

"What do you think?" Dewey and Louie ask Huey.
"I **LOVE** it!" says Huey. "Turns out there are lots of ways to help others and be kind."

Everyone cheers! And everyone agrees: **you can't have too much kindness!**